Ginger

Saddle Up Series
Book 27

D0646042

Dave and Pat Sargent are longtime residents of Prairie Grove, Arkansas. Dave, a fourth-generation dairy farmer, began writing in early December of 1990. Pat, a former teacher, began writing in the fourth grade. They enjoy the outdoors and have a real love for animals.

Ginger

Saddle Up Series
Book 27

By Dave and Pat Sargent

Beyond "The End"
By Sue Rogers

Illustrated by Jane Lenoir

Ozark Publishing, Inc.
P.O. Box 228
Prairie Grove, AR 72753

Cataloging-in-Publication Data

Sargent, Dave, 1941—
   Ginger / by Dave and Pat Sargent ;
illustrated by Jane Lenoir.—Prairie Grove, AR :
Ozark Publishing, c2004.
     p. cm. (Saddle up series ; 27)

     "Be likeable"—Cover.
    SUMMARY: Ginger, a lilac roan horse,
is chosen by a young telegrapher named
Thomas Edison to accompany him on his
exploration of the Midwest as he considers
what to do with his life. Includes factual
information about lilac roan horses.
     ISBN 1-56763-811-2 (hc)
          1-56763-812-0 (pbk)

    1. Horses—Juvenile fiction. [1. Horses—
Fiction. 2. Edison, Thomas A. (Thomas Alva),
1847–1931—Fiction. 3. Inventors—Fiction.
4. West (U.S.)—Fiction.] I. Sargent, Pat, 1936–
II. Lenoir, Jane, 1950– ill. III. Title. IV. Series.

    PZ7.S2465Gf 2004
    [Fic]—dc21   2001008641

iv

Inspired by

lilac roans we have seen as we travel across the many states we visit.

Dedicated to

all schoolchildren
who have a good attitude.

Foreword

Ginger is a pretty lilac roan with a good attitude. Her boss is Thomas Edison. She respects his intelligence and believes that he will be talked about in history books as a great inventor of new and wonderful ideas. But his latest project is a hard one. He calls it an electric lamp.

Contents

If you would like to have the authors of the Saddle Up Series visit your school, free of charge, call 1-800-321-5671 or 1-800-960-3876.

One

The Lilac Roan

The sun was peeking over the eastern horizon as a big team of horses pulling a wagon arrived at the Rocking S Horse Ranch. Ginger the lilac roan raised her head, and her ears shot forward. "Hmmm," she thought. "We have early morning guests. I wonder what they're doing at this early hour."

"Welcome to the Rocking S," she nickered. "My name is Ginger."

"Thanks, Ginger," said the big bay sabino hitched to the wagon.

"We have traveled many miles, and it will be nice to rest for a while."

"Yes, it will," the grey sabino agreed. "Our boss and his three friends have been a lot of fun on this trip, but I'm getting a bit tired."

The team winked at Ginger and one of them said with a chuckle, "We'll try to look pitiful so that our boss will stay here for a while."

Ginger nodded her head and smiled.

"Just lower your heads and breathe heavily," she said with a laugh. "That should get his attention."

She nodded her head at the team as the ranch foreman shook hands with one of the strangers in the wagon.

"Welcome to the Rocking S," he said. "What can we do for you?"

The newcomer stepped off the wagon and removed his hat. He

said, "My name is Thomas Edison. I'm looking for a good horse to roam the western countryside with me. Do you have an easy-going, likeable horse that would fit my needs?"

"Yessir, Mr. Edison," the ranch foreman replied. "I'm sure we have the perfect horse partner for you. But why don't you and your friends come into the house and have some breakfast with us before we talk business?"

"Hmmm," Ginger nickered. "I'm proud to live on the Rocking S. This ranch is known far and wide for its hospitality and friendly folks."

"We thank you, sir," Thomas said with a big smile of appreciation. "I am one telegrapher who likes to start the day with a good breakfast, and we haven't had one for several days. I believe that breakfast is the most important meal of the day."

"Hey!" the bay sabino snorted. "How about us? We're tired, and we're hungry, too."

One of the men on the wagon laughed and slapped the lines against his rump.

"Okay, sabinos," he said with a chuckle. "Let's take the wagon to the barn, and I'll unhitch you for a while. Then you can eat some hay and drink some water while we talk business."

"That sounds like a winner," the grey sabino whinnied.

"Yes, it does," Ginger agreed. "Welcome to my corral, fellows."

Two hours later, the foreman brought Thomas Edison and his friends to the corral. As they stood beside the fence looking at the herd of horses, the bay sabino suddenly stomped his front hoof on the ground and nickered.

"Ginger, do something cute to get their attention. Mr. Edison is looking at that silver dun, and we want him to choose you."

"I can't. I don't know how to do anything cute," she whinnied.

"Prance up to him and nicker," the bay sabino suggested. "At least he'll see you."

"Yeah, that's a good idea," the grey sabino said with a nod of his head. "And if that doesn't do it, give him a kiss on his cheek with your upper lip. He always likes that. That's what I do when he's upset with me."

"Well, I guess I can do that," Ginger said with a giggle. "As a matter of fact, this may be fun!"

"Now!" the sabino whispered. "Do it now!"

Moments later, the lilac roan took a deep breath and raised her head. She trotted and pranced in a circle in front of the men. Her thick mane and tail swayed gently with the graceful movement of her body.

Thomas Edison smiled and then nodded his head.

"That lilac roan is a pretty little mare," he said. Then he pointed to the silver dun and added, "But he's a good-looking horse, too. I just can't decide which one to take."

Ginger suddenly stopped her prancing. She walked slowly toward Thomas Edison. She stomped her right front hoof on the ground as she halted in front of him. And a second later, her upper lip was nuzzling him on the cheek.

"Okay," he said with pleasure in his voice. "I love a horse with a good attitude. Mr. Ranch Foreman, I want to purchase this little lilac roan. She has winning ways."

Ginger winked at the two big sabinos.

"Great! Thanks for your help, fellows," she nickered softly.

Two

Boss Thomas Edison

Ginger Lilac Roan immediately loved her new boss. Each evening as he fed her, he spoke of his early memories.

"When I was just a young boy," he told her quietly, "I was trying to hop on a freight train. A trainman grabbed me by my ears and pulled me on board. I truly believe that is the reason I do not hear well today," he confided.

Ginger gently rubbed her nose against his chest and nickered softly.

"I'm sorry that you don't hear very well, Boss. But, don't worry. I'll take good care of you." After traveling three days with the two sabinos through the Piney Woods of east Texas, the men in the wagon decided to return to their homes.

"What are you going to do, Thomas?" one of the men asked.

He smiled and patted the pretty lilac roan on her neck as he said, "Ginger and I are going to travel through the midwest for a while. I would like to see some new country. We will follow the telegraph lines, and I'll always be able to find a job when we need some money."

"You're right," his friend on the wagon agreed. "Telegraphers are always in demand. Good luck to you, Thomas. We'll see you when you and Ginger get tired of roaming the countryside and want to come home for a while."

"Maybe I will know what to do with my life by then," Mr. Edison added with a chuckle. "I can't seem to figure out exactly what profession I should be doing."

Ginger nuzzled him on the cheek and nickered softly, "That's okay, Boss. We'll find your talent, and I'm sure you'll be excellent in your chosen work."

That night Ginger and Thomas set up camp by themselves for the first time. As Thomas sat down beside the little campfire, the faithful lilac roan stood quietly beside him.

After a long period of silence, Thomas suddenly cleared his throat and said, "Ginger, I've been hearing a lot about electricity lately. Maybe I should study that idea and learn to use it."

"Yeah, Boss," she murmured sleepily, "maybe you should. Now, let's get some sleep, okay?"

For two months, Ginger and Thomas slowly traveled north and west.

One afternoon as they stopped on top of a big hill, a sudden bolt of lightning pierced the darkening sky.

It was so unexpected that both the lilac roan and Thomas jumped.

"Wow! Did you see that, Boss? Where did that lightning come from? I haven't even heard any thunder."

Seconds later a thick layer of smoke drifted upward from the extremely dry Nebraska grasslands. Ginger pointed a front hoof toward the flames and neighed loudly.

"Look, Boss! That sudden bolt of lightning started a prairie fire!"

Thomas nudged her gently in the ribs as he reined her toward the flames.

"We must put it out, Ginger," he yelled. "A prairie fire will kill every animal and person in its path."

The lilac roan skidded to a halt several yards from the already hot flames. Thomas quickly dismounted and uncinched the saddle. He tossed it on the ground, then grabbed the saddle blanket and began beating out the flames with it.

Ginger stomped at the glowing embers with her front hooves.

Time passed unnoticed by horse and man as they desperately fought to stop the prairie fire. Then Ginger saw Thomas staggering and gasping for breath. "Uh-oh," she thought. "Boss is going to pass out if I don't do something quick."

"Boss!" she neighed. "We have to get to safety. This fire is too big for us to handle. We need to get to a safe place immediately."

Thomas fell to his knees, and a moment later he was sprawled on the singed grass. Ginger ran to his side and knelt down.

"Get on my back, Boss," she neighed. "Hurry!"

When he didn't respond, she reached around and clamped down on his belt with her teeth. Then she gently shoved him across her back.

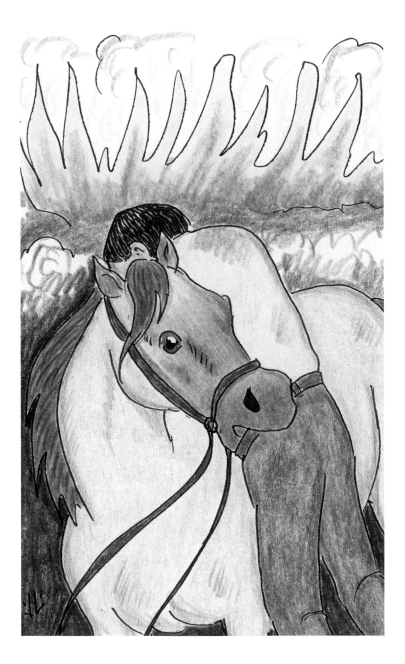

"Hang on, Boss," she muttered. "I saw a river in the valley below. If we can make it to the river, we're going for a swim."

Three

Electric Lamps? Wow!

The lilac roan raced across the Nebraska grasslands with Thomas balanced on her back. A huge cloud of dark smoke covered the western horizon as they moved ever closer to the big river below. Finally reaching the bank, Ginger stepped carefully into the slow-moving water. As the cold liquid touched Thomas Edison's body, he regained consciousness and his strength.

"Are you feeling better, Boss?" Ginger nickered. "Are you okay?"

Thomas washed his face before sliding off the lilac roan's back and wading to the southern bank.

"I'll be okay now, Ginger," he
said. "I need to rest for a moment."

She watched him lie down on
the grass before slowly wading from
the river and walking toward him.

"You're safe now, Boss," she murmured. "Maybe you should try to get a little sleep now. I'll stand guard over you while you rest."

Seconds later, his gentle snore joined the sound of the river. "Hmmm," Ginger thought as she looked down at him. "It's about time for Boss to settle down. This roaming through the countryside is too dangerous for him. I know he has a special destiny in life. I'll just take care of him until he finds it."

In October of 1868, Ginger and Thomas Edison knew his destiny.

"I want to be an inventor, my dear Ginger," he said as he filed patent papers for the first time. "I'm sure that lots of new ideas have not been discovered yet, and I'm just the man to find them."

"You're right, Boss!" Ginger said excitedly. "You just invented an electric vote recorder, and I know this is only the beginning of your new and exciting career."

Thomas nodded his head and said, "I have a great idea for a better stock ticker."

"Humph, Boss," the lilac roan grunted. "I know you'll do more with your inventions than that. Why don't you work on something like an automatic telegraph system? Since you are no longer a telegrapher, making an automatic one won't hurt your chances for a job."

Days passed into months as Ginger and Thomas explored new ideas for new inventions.

Early one evening Ginger was waiting for Thomas at the hitching post when a blue-eyed palomino stopped beside her.

"Good evening," Ginger said with a smile. "Is your boss an inventor, too?"

The blue-eyed palomino threw back his head and snorted, "No. Your boss is the boss of my boss."

Ginger pointed one ear forward and the other one back. She shook her head and pawed the ground with one front hoof.

After shaking her head for a few seconds, she said, "I don't understand all of that boss stuff. Just tell me, is your boss an inventor?" she repeated.

"No," the blue-eyed palomino said gruffly. "My boss is called a mathematician, and he works for your boss."

"Oh," Ginger said quietly. "Now I understand."

Suddenly her eyes sparkled with excitement.

"Our bosses are working on an idea for a new lamp, aren't they?"

"Well, that may be right," the palomino said. "My boss said that Thomas Edison is trying to make a lamp light out of electricity. But that sounds pretty dumb to me."

"Hmmm," Ginger said aloud. "You could look at it from my point of view. Electricity makes light. Lightning makes light. It sounds pretty smart to me."

The blue-eyed palomino looked at Ginger for a long time. Finally, he nodded his head.

"I see what you mean, Ginger. When you explain it that way, it all makes sense."

Ginger the lilac roan smiled and pranced around for a few seconds.

"Just wait, my friend. My boss, Mr. Thomas Edison, will be written about in history books someday.

He'll be famous for his wonderful inventions that will help the entire world!"

"Hmmm," she thought. "I wonder if folks will remember his lilac roan horse named Ginger."

"It doesn't matter," she said with a giggle. "Life is full of new and wonderful ideas and exciting times!"

Four

Lilac Roan Facts

Roan is a mixture of colored and white hairs. The head and points on a roan have colored hairs only.

Roans are born roan and shed roan. We have never seen a roan dappled. Although grey horses fit the general classification of roan, greys are born solid colored and get lighter as they age.

Roans are lightest in the spring. They look white, with dark points. They get darker in the summer and they are darkest in the winter.

Lilac roans have the same roan pattern as do dark chestnuts or liver chestnuts. They are beautiful horses.

Lilac Roan

BEYOND "THE END"

Horses want one place rubbed—
themselves!
Anonymous

WORD LIST
  lilac roan
  phonograph
  nostril
  bay sabino
  antiseptic solution
  electric light bulb
  cheek
  carbon button transmitter
  grey sabino
  clinical thermometer
  mimeograph
  withers
  blue-eyed palomino
  kinetograph

hock
bandages
kinetoscope
chocolate chestnut
pastern
first talking movie picture
cotton wool

From the word list above, write:

1. Four words that name first aid supplies that should be kept in one place.
2. Five words that are color names for horses.
3. Five words that name points on a horse.
4. Seven words that name inventions made by Thomas Edison.

What are carbon button transmitters used in (even today)? What was a kinetograph? What was a kinetoscope?

CURRICULUM CONNECTIONS

Thomas Edison patented 1,093 discoveries! Would you believe, because of hearing problems, he was not a good student—but he read every book he could find? To thank him for saving the life of his young son, a man taught him how to use the telegraph.

Edison invented many things for the telegraph. What were the first words he recorded when he invented the tinfoil phonograph? (Hint: He recited a nursery rhyme. Which one?)

See a picture of Thomas Edison, see his signature, see pictures of the first gramophone, hear his first recording, hear his recorded voice telling about the light bulb, and learn other interesting things at website <www.cyg.net/ ~jhall/gphone. html>.

The ranch foreman invited Thomas Edison and his friends to come in and have breakfast. Mr. Edison said that breakfast was the most important meal of the day, and he was right!

Instead of a bowl of cold cereal packed with sugar, or a sweet roll for your breakfast everyday, try one of the breakfast ideas at <www.childrensrecipes.com>. Maybe have Texas Sunshine or Ham Hash instead! There are four new recipes every week. YUMM!!

PROJECT

Combine your math and artistic skills! Draw to scale and accurately color a picture (body, tail, and mane) of the horse that is featured in each book read in the Saddle Up Series. You could soon have sixty horses prancing around the walls of your classroom!
Learning + horses = FUN.

Look in your school library media center for books about how to draw a horse and the colors of horses. Don't forget the useful information in the last chapter of this book (Lilac Roan Facts) and the picture on the book cover for a shape and color guide.

HELPFUL HINTS AND WEBSITES
A horse is measured in hands. One hand equals four inches. Use a scale of 1" equals 1 hand.

41

Visit website <www.equisearch.com> to find a glossary of equine terms, information about tack and equipment, breeds, art and graphics, and more about horses. Learn more at <www.horse-country. com> and at <www.ansi.okstate.edu/ breeds/horses/>.

KidsClick! is a web search for kids by librarians. There are many interesting websites here. HORSES and HORSE-MANSHIP are two of the more than 600 subjects. Visit <www.kidsclick.org>.

Is your classroom beginning to look like the Rocking S Horse Ranch? Happy Trails to You!

ANSWERS (1. telephone speakers and microphones. 2. motion picture camera. 3. motion picture viewer.)